Reaction

Reaction

Lesley Choyce

orca soundings

ORCA BOOK PUBLISHERS

National Library of Canada Cataloguing in Publication Data

Choyce, Lesley, 1951-

Reaction / written by Lesley Choyce.

(Orca soundings)

ISBN 978-1-55469-278-1 (bound).--ISBN 978-1-55469-277-4 (pbk.)

I. Title. II. Series: Orca soundings

PS8555.H668R42 2010   jC813'.54   C2009-906847-8

First published in the United States, 2010

Library of Congress Control Number: 2009940838

Summary: When Zach finds out that his girlfriend is pregnant,
he is terrified. What will they do?

Orca Book Publishers gratefully acknowledges the support for its publishing
programs provided by the following agencies: the Government of Canada
through the Canada Book Fund and the Canada Council for the Arts,
and the Province of British Columbia through the BC Arts Council
and the Book Publishing Tax Credit.

Cover design by Teresa Bubela
Cover photography by Getty Images

ORCA BOOK PUBLISHERS
PO Box 5626, STN. B
VICTORIA, BC Canada
V8R 6S4

ORCA BOOK PUBLISHERS
PO Box 468
CUSTER, WA USA
98240-0468

www.orcabook.com
Printed and bound in Canada.
Printed on 100% PCW recycled paper.

13   12   11   10 • 4 3 2 1

Chapter One

"Zach, I'm pregnant."

Ashley dropped the bombshell on me between classes at school. I remember the exact time, because I was standing in front of the hallway clock. 11:11. Yep. Eleven eleven in the morning. It was a Tuesday.

She was looking straight at me when she blurted it right out.

1

"That's impossible," I snapped back. And I looked away from her and back to the stupid clock. The time changed to 11:12.

"It's true," she said. And then she began to cry.

I put my arm around her and pulled her toward me. "Let's go," I said.

"Where?"

"Anywhere. Let's get out of here."

I led her down the hall and out the front door into the bright sunlight. As I opened the door of the school, I had this feeling that maybe nothing in my life would ever be the same again.

That was exactly how it happened. I will never forget the feeling. I had never been more scared in my life. Never. I know that I wasn't the first guy to hear those words from his girlfriend, but it felt that way. Sad to say, I wasn't even thinking about Ashley at the time. I was thinking about me. What was I going to do? What was going to happen to me? What would this do to my life?

We walked for almost an hour. Neither of us talked at first. Then I began to rationalize, and one part of my brain wanted to convince us both that it must be some kind of mistake.

"Are you sure?" I asked.

"Yes."

"How sure?"

"Very sure."

"Maybe you made a mistake."

"Maybe *we* made a mistake," she said.

"I mean, about the tests. Did you buy one of those testing things from the drugstore?"

"Three of them."

"Maybe they were defective."

"They were three different brands. They all had the same results."

I was still looking for a way out of this. I was looking for a way to get *me* out of this. I almost asked her if she was sure it was me, that I was the father. But I didn't.

Because just then I remembered. Two months ago. We'd been partying. (That's what we did, Ashley and I. We partied big-time.) We'd been drinking. And my parents were gone for the weekend. And one thing led to another. And we were so into it.

And I knew the condom broke, but I didn't mention a word to her. Hey, I thought it would wreck the mood. Plus, what were the chances?

So there I was, sixteen years old, walking through the suburban streets with my fifteen-year-old girlfriend who has just told me she's pregnant. And I'm still thinking, this can't be happening to me.

"I'm scared," Ashley said, leaning into me and holding tightly onto my arm.

I didn't tell her how scared I was, and I didn't even tell her about the condom then. I said what guys say in situations like this when the blood has drained out of their heads and they are screaming inside, panicking, ready to run for the hills and never come back. I said, "Everything is going to be all right."

Chapter Two

The morning became the afternoon, and it started to sink in. Ashley was two months pregnant. We had been going out together for only three months. She seemed to be sold on me. And I loved being with her. She was sweet and sexy and one year younger than me, which should have been no big deal. But one year can sometimes seem like a big issue in high school. She had been flattered that I wanted to hang out with her—most of the time it was just the two of us—and, well, like I said, she was sweet and sexy.

We ended up sitting on a bench in a park where mothers pushed their little kids on swings and bigger kids played on the slide and the monkey bars. There were babies in strollers and mothers chatting about brands of throwaway diapers. It was the worst place to be thinking about Ashley being pregnant, but it's like the gods had planned it this way.

Ashley cried, and I held her. She stopped and then started crying again, and some of those mothers looked at us—some seemed concerned, and some scowled. I just held her and wondered how one minute everything can be okay and the next, everything has changed.

I don't know why I didn't keep my mouth shut. I felt I had to say something.

I guess I felt she needed to have an explanation. So I told her about the broken condom.

And that changed everything.

Ashley pulled away. The expression changed on her face. "Why didn't you say something that night?"

Yes, why didn't I? I shrugged.

"Then this is all your fault," she said, way too loud.

"I'm sorry. It's no good getting mad at me now. We have to figure out what to do," I said unconvincingly.

"If I had known, I could have maybe done something."

"I know," I said. I knew she was referring to morning-after pills. I just didn't think at the time that one little slipup would result in this.

"I trusted you," she said.

"I know," I said, hanging my head.

"You bastard," she snapped back. And then she hit me.

Well, it could have been a slap. I'm not sure. Something between a slap and a punch right on the side of my face. Then she got up and started walking away. I ignored the stinging in my face and followed her. All eyes in the park, even those of the little kids, were on us.

"Please, wait," I pleaded. Ashley shook me off and just kept walking. She turned once to say, "I never want to speak to you again," before walking off into the afternoon.

I was dizzy, and I was having a hard time getting my bearings. I didn't know what to do. A voice in my brain kept telling me to go after her, but instead I turned and walked home. I told my mom I was sick, and I went to my bedroom and played *Guitar Hero*. I know how that sounds, but that's what I did. I ate a silent supper when the time came, played some more

Guitar Hero and then went to sleep feeling like crap. I kept trying to think of some way out of this. Some plan. But all I did was keep beating myself up. What had I been thinking? Was sex really so important that I let this happen? Eventually I fell asleep.

When I woke in the morning, the problem was still there, staring me square in the face.

Chapter Three

Over the next few days, things went from bad to worse. Ashley walked away from me every time I tried to talk to her. She had two words for me: "Get away." That's all she'd say. And each time my heart sank. Her brother Stephen followed me into the bathroom one afternoon. Stephen was my age and in many of my classes. He was a big guy, a wrestler on the school team, and legendary for his bad temper, which I think he got from his father.

"You're gonna have to watch your back from now on," he said in a voice that sounded like he'd been gargling with Drano. We were standing side by side at the urinals. Before we were done, he turned and pissed on my shoes and then walked out the door.

I knew that Ashley and her brother were close, but I was surprised to think that she would have told him she was pregnant. But, as I was cleaning my shoes, it occurred to me that she didn't have to tell him she was pregnant. All she had to do was make up anything about me that would get Stephen angry enough to, well, piss on my shoes. Damn.

It wasn't long before I started to get the picture. Some of Ashley's friends started giving me dirty looks. Her brother reappeared when I was waiting for the bus and "accidentally" shoved me in line so that I rammed into a couple of kids in front of me.

Gossip travels fast in school, and before long I was getting dirty looks from people I didn't even know. I started to avoid looking at anyone in the hallways. At home, *Guitar Hero* wasn't enough of an escape to avoid thinking about my problem.

When some of the girls started calling me "The Perv," I didn't know how to react. It was starting to get to me, so when Elisse, a girl I once considered my friend, glared at me, I stopped her in the hall. I still couldn't believe that Ashley had told everyone she was pregnant. It had to be something else.

"What is it?" I asked her. "Why does everyone suddenly hate me?"

Elisse continued to glare at me. She started to walk away, so I grabbed her, and this made her even angrier.

"What is it?" I repeated.

"You mean, you don't know?"

"No. Help me here."

"We all know that you forced Ashley Walker into having sex with you. You perv."

She twisted herself away and walked off, turning once to glare yet again and, this time, give me the finger.

So this was Ashley's revenge. Yes, we'd had sex. And apparently I got her pregnant. But I would never, ever, try to force myself on any girl. Never.

So now I had two problems. But they were two damn big problems, and it felt more like a hundred. I needed someone that I could talk to. I decided I had to confide in someone—not my parents and not any of my so-called friends. But who was I kidding? I didn't have that many friends anyway. It would have to be Kiley. She was one of my ex-girlfriends. Kiley was always the smart one and so cute. I was surprised that she had even been interested in me. She was out of my league. But I kept doing stupid things around her. Like that party I convinced her to have at her parents' house, where I puked in the living room. And that other party where she found me off in a corner kissing a girl whose name I can't even remember. She had plenty of good reasons for dumping me. But strangely enough, she stayed friends with me after we broke up.

After school that day, I found Kiley at the bus stop. I followed her on. She sat down in the back, and I sat down beside her. It was just the two of us on the back seat. I was afraid she was going to give me that look all the other girls were giving me. She didn't, although she didn't look all that happy to see me.

"Hi," I said.

"Hi." She looked puzzled.

"Aren't you going to ask me how I'm doing?"

"I know how you're doing," she said. "You've been voted most-hated student at the school. You're human garbage. I imagine that doesn't feel so good."

"But what people think isn't true," I said. "Ashley is mad at me…for something else…so she spread this rumor."

Kiley nodded. "I think I knew that. I know you're not that kind of guy. Horny, yes, but not...well, like that."

"Thank you."

"Everyone believes what they want to believe. But then why is Ashley so mad at you?" she asked.

"Can I trust you?"

"Trust me to what? Keep a secret? I don't know."

So I told her anyway. Kiley's eyes grew wide. "This is not good."

"What am I going to do?"

"Well, the first thing you have to do is talk to her. It's no good for her to stay mad at you. You have to discuss options."

"Yeah, right. Options."

"You need to figure out what is best for both of you," Kiley said.

"What *is* best for us?" I asked.

"I can't say that, you know that, Zach. Remember when we broke up? We both knew it was the best thing for both of us. We talked and we both decided."

"Yeah, but this is different."

"Still, you need to sit down and talk to her," she said. "This is not about you right now. This is about her."

And I guess it sank in just then. All along, I had still been thinking about how bad this all was for me. This must be even worse for Ashley.

Chapter Four

I needed to talk to Ashley. Some days after school she went to a coffee shop close to her house. She usually went with a group of friends. They would all no doubt hate my guts, but I'd have to take that chance. I hopped off the bus at Kiley's stop and ran ten blocks to Java Junction. I was winded when I opened the door and spotted her.

Not giving myself time to catch my breath, I went right over to her table. The conversation stopped dead. "I'm sorry, Ashley," I said. "I'm sorry. I'll do anything you want me to do. Anything. Please."

I stood there for an awkward minute. I waited for her to say something, but she didn't. Everyone else just stared at me.

I didn't know what else to say. I tried to slow the pounding of my heart. Looking at her, I realized that something had changed in the way she looked at me. The anger was gone. It was replaced by confusion. "Anything," I repeated, as if that word would do the trick. And maybe I should have stopped there and turned around, but instead I kept going. "I love you," I added.

I watched her face for a response. It caught her totally off guard. It caught me off guard too. We'd had fun together and got along really well. But it was only now sinking in that I cared for this girl. I think I loved her.

And now we were both scared. There was dead silence. Then she stood up, and I saw the look on her face change from confusion back to anger. And she blurted it out. "Bullshit!" she said. "Liar." The other girls scowled at me.

I had failed in my mission. I turned and headed out the door. All I could think about was getting out of there.

I hadn't realized that she had followed me outside until I reached the corner and felt a hand grab my shoulder and twist me around. "I'm going to have this taken care of, and I want you to pay for it."

I'd thought about this but wasn't sure it was the right thing to do. "We need to talk first. Is this really what you want?"

She didn't answer that question. Instead she said, "My friends think you can be criminally charged. They say I should go to the police."

"That would be crazy. Ashley, I'm sorry about all this. We need to go talk to somebody who can help us sort this out. Not the police."

"Nobody can help us. You screwed up everything. I want you punished."

"Is that why you lied and told people I forced you to have sex with me? You know it wasn't that way." Ashley didn't answer. She just stared at me. I felt trapped, and my mind froze.

Then she took out her cell phone and started to make a call. "Who are you calling?" I asked, my voice shaking.

"My parents," she said.

I didn't know what else to do. I turned my back on her, and I began to run.

Chapter Five

I was never much of a runner. I ran for three blocks until my lungs felt like they were about to burst. I was afraid to go home. Afraid the police might actually be there. I didn't know much about the law. If a sixteen-year-old guy has sex with a girl only one year younger, could that be a crime? And if it was, what would they do to me?

Everyone would know. And everyone would hate me. And my parents? What would they think of their son?

It was beginning to sink in that I could be in real trouble. That scared the crap out of me. And none of this seemed fair. Was it really all my fault? It wasn't like Ashley and I were the only ones having sex. So why did everyone want to blame me? Now I was feeling angry. All I wanted to do was get away from it all.

I caught a bus that took me to one of the main highways out of town. And, for the first time in my life, I stuck out my thumb there on the ramp leading up into the traffic. All I could think about was leaving. Leaving and maybe never coming back.

A guy in a van picked me up and drove me a half hour out of town, all the while talking about baseball and politics. A second driver, a guy in his early twenties who looked like he was high, took me farther up into the mountains. The music was loud, and he didn't speak to me the whole time. When we came to a river with a waterfall, I asked him to let me out there.

As I climbed down the embankment, I tried to calm myself. I hiked away from the highway along the raging river and sat at the base of the waterfall. It seemed both frightening, with all that power, but also beautiful. I took a deep breath and suddenly felt kind of giddy.

I had escaped. I had taken the first step in just leaving all that crap behind. I could do this. I could just disappear. Go somewhere else where no one knew me and no one would find me. Forget about Ashley and the stupid pregnancy. Forget about what everyone back there thought of me.

It would be that easy.

The giddiness lasted for almost an hour. And then the doubt set in.

I scooped some of the icy cold water into my hands and splashed it onto my face once and then twice.

And then reality slammed back into me like a freight train.

Could I do this to my parents? Did I really want to leave everything behind?

Yes, maybe I could do this if I had to. But not yet. Not now. I felt vulnerable. I'd only been gone a few hours, and I was already feeling lost and lonely. It would be dark soon. Then what? I felt like a lost little boy.

The hitchhiking back home wasn't so easy. I think the first driver who stopped, a middle-aged woman with sunglasses, was drunk. She slurred her speech. The next driver turned out to be a church minister who kept asking me what was wrong. I didn't tell him. It took three more short rides, each after a long wait, to get me back to my neighborhood.

I'd missed dinner, and my mom and dad wanted to know where I'd been.

"You've been acting weird," my dad said. "Want to tell us what's wrong?" My dad's an okay guy, just a little old-school. Always did everything by the book. How could I answer him?

And my mom. She stood there looking so worried. I knew that she'd never approved of Ashley. Maybe it was the age thing. Maybe something else. They were both good parents. I hated doing this to them, but I was going crazy keeping my problems to myself. So I said it.

"I got Ashley pregnant."

I saw the muscles in my father's jaw tighten. I saw the shock in his eyes.

And my mom—she sucked in a gasp of air and then looked quickly away out the window.

I went upstairs to my bedroom and lay on my bed. Ten minutes later my mom and dad came in with my dinner and watched in awkward silence as I took a few bites. Finally, my father cleared his throat and asked, "Have the two of you gone to speak to a doctor or someone at Planned Parenthood? You have options, you know."

There was that word.

"I'm not sure Ashley will talk to me."

"Call her," my mom said. "Talk to her."

After they left me alone, I did call her. And, amazingly, she did not hang up.

"I nearly ran away today. For good."

"Why did you come back?" I didn't hear any anger in her voice.

"I don't know. I just couldn't leave."

"What you said today in the coffee shop, was it true?"

I took a deep breath. I couldn't lie to her. "I don't know. I'm not even sure I know what love is. I just know that I do care what happens to you. I know it's my fault, but I'd like to be there for you."

"I'm not sure what to say. One minute I hate you and the next I want to be with you. It's like an emotional roller coaster."

"I know," I said.

"What do you want us to do?"

"I want us to go together to Planned Parenthood. I want to find some stuff out. Okay?"

There was a long dead silence on the line.

Then she said, "Okay."

Chapter Six

We went to the clinic the next day after school. Neither of us told our parents. We were both nervous, but the clinic staff treated us okay. We sat in a room with a lady doctor. She said her name was Dr. Benson. She seemed nice enough, and you could tell she'd done this a thousand times before. I tried to hold Ashley's hand, but she pulled away. I think it was just the nerves. This was hard on both of us.

"You could have a procedure," the doctor said, "if this is not the right time. If you really don't want to have a baby, we can schedule you in. I'm not advising you to do this. It's just that the earlier it's done, the simpler the procedure is." She paused. "The other option, of course, is that you can have the baby. Then you could put it up for adoption. There are a lot of married women out there who can't get pregnant. To them, it would be a blessing."

"What if we didn't want to give it up?" I heard myself blurt out. The room went silent, and Ashley looked at me like I'd lost my mind.

"I'm just saying, what if?" I added.

The doctor cleared her throat. "It's an option," she said. "This is all about choices—your choices. What's best for you both and what's best for the baby. If there is a baby."

Ashley took my hand now but didn't look at me. "When do we have to decide?" she said.

"The sooner, the better," Dr. Benson said. "Just be sure you decide on something you can follow through on. Something you can live with."

When we left the office, we didn't say anything to each other. I think we were in shock. I walked Ashley home and tried to start a conversation—first about the decision, but then anything just to fill the dead air. Each time Ashley said the same thing: "I can't talk about this right now."

As we approached her house, she said, "I'm okay from here. You go on home. Let's sleep on this and see what things look like tomorrow."

I nodded and gave her a hug. I knew she didn't want me anywhere near her house or her parents. Best to keep a low profile, I thought.

I slept terribly that night. I'd doze off and then wake back up. At school the next day, Ashley still looked like she was in shock and didn't want to talk to me about the clinic or the decision. I got that. I didn't want to talk about it either. On my second near-sleepless night, I got up and sat down at my computer. I visited websites on teenage pregnancy and abortion. Pro and con. I tried to stay away from the sites where people expressed strong views one way or the other. I wanted this to be our decision. Ashley's and mine. Man, there were a lot of strongly opinionated people out there on this topic. I didn't know who was right or who was wrong. And I didn't know what I thought about it myself. I guess there were a lot of things I was uncertain about.

Then I googled *teen fathers*. It was weird just keying in the words. I mean really weird.

I ended up at a website in New Zealand, of all places. Teenage guys had posted their stories about being fathers. Now I was wide-awake. Some of them were eighteen and nineteen. Some of them younger. One guy was only fifteen. They wrote about how difficult it was. Some of them had been pushed away by the girl or her parents and were angry. A couple of the older guys had actually moved in with the girl and the baby and were trying to make it on their own. They were struggling. But a couple of younger guys had decided to just stay in the picture. Both parents were still going to school, both lived at home. They sure as hell didn't have it easy. But these guys were committed to being the baby's father. One guy named Mark made it sound like it wasn't so bad, and he seemed totally committed to being there to help his girlfriend and to be a good father.

I read every posting on that site. There were pictures—some with the mother and father. Some with just the dad and the baby. There was even one dude who was raising his kid at home with his own parents. After the baby was born, the girl had said she wanted nothing to do with him or the baby. None of the stories suggested anything was easy.

I kept wondering why and how these guys had been able to go this route. Man, it must have been damn hard. But some of them seemed proud of being a father. They were helping to raise their own kid. One part of me thought that was awesome. But the reality of such a decision was starting to kick in. Helping to raise a baby. Being there for a little kid who is growing up. Just thinking about it made me shake. This was all getting way too weird.

Chapter Seven

I don't exactly know why I did what I did next. It was nearly midnight when I woke up my parents. "I need to talk," I said. I had already told my parents about the meeting with the counselor at Planned Parenthood, and they had been surprisingly cool about it all. I think they were pretty sure we would get the abortion, but they weren't pushing me one way or the other. Now I was having second thoughts.

"What's wrong, Zach?" my mom asked, sitting bolt upright and suddenly fully awake.

I sat down on the edge of their bed and suddenly felt like a little kid again, coming into my parents' room in the middle of the night because I was scared. "I've been thinking," I said. I swallowed hard and then continued. "I've been thinking about Ashley and about her being pregnant."

"We know it's not easy," my mom interrupted, trying to sound comforting.

My father rubbed his eyes and tried to focus on me. "What is it, Zach?"

I swallowed hard. "What if we decide not to have the abortion?"

My mom turned on the table lamp to look at my face. They both looked a little stunned.

My father cleared his throat. "I thought the two of you went to the clinic to talk to the doctor about…well, having a procedure to, um, terminate the pregnancy."

"We did. I'm just not a hundred percent sure it's the right thing for us."

"What does Ashley think?"

"I haven't talked to her yet about this. I mean we've talked about a possible abortion or her having the baby and giving it up. But what I'm thinking about is different."

"I just don't see how it could work," my father snapped and was about to say more, but my mom touched his arm. He didn't say anything else.

"I think you need to have a serious talk with Ashley," my mother said.

"I know. I just didn't want to phone her. I need to do this face-to-face."

"Of course," she said. My dad still looked a little stunned.

I waited until lunchtime the next day. I stood by the cafeteria door until Ashley came along with a couple of her friends. She looked a little pale. The two other girls just glared at me. Around school, I didn't know what to expect from anyone. Many of my classmates knew something or thought they knew something about me—I just didn't know what. Maybe some knew the truth, and others had been told a bunch of bullshit about me. I was tired of the looks I was getting.

"Ashley, can we talk?" I asked. "Alone," I added.

Ashley nodded okay. "I'm not feeling all that great. I don't think I can eat anything."

This made me feel more than a little guilty. "I'm sorry," I said.

"It's okay. Let's go over to that empty table by the window."

Everybody stared as we walked across the room. The lunchtime music was blasting away. We sat down by the window.

Ashley spoke first. "My parents think terminating the pregnancy now while it's still early is the way to go. They've backed off on talking to the police about having you charged."

I didn't even want to think about the legal side of things. I didn't believe anyone would really have me charged with a crime. But then, what did I know?

"I think my dad feels that's the way to go too," I said.

"It's the easy way out," Ashley said. "For you at least." There was an edge to her voice when she said that last part.

"What about you? What do you want?"

"I still don't know. It's too big of a decision. I can't make up my mind."

"Do you want to know what I think?" I asked.

"Well, yeah," she said. "But I'm almost afraid to ask."

I didn't just blurt it out. I told her about my conversation with my parents. And I told her about the website. I told her about the stories of the teen dads, and that I had even emailed the guy named Mark, who had posted his contact info after his story. By this morning, he had sent me a response. *Having the baby and being there for my son was the smartest and most important thing I ever did in life*, Mark had written.

Ashley looked puzzled. "You're taking advice from someone you don't even know, who is on the other side of the planet?"

"That's not it," I countered. "It's just that it is such an important decision and I'm trying to figure out what is right."

She looked a little sick again, and she turned her head away from me and just stared out the window.

I left things there hanging in the air for a minute, wishing the damn music wasn't so loud. Finally I asked, "What are you thinking?"

"I'm thinking I want my life back. I want to go back to being just a girl going to high school. I wish this never happened. I wish I never met you." There was no anger in her voice.

"I'm glad I met you," I said. "I think we can do this thing together."

She was still staring out the window, and I saw tears begin to form in her eyes. And then she turned to me. And she kissed me. She held my face in her hands and kissed me like she meant it.

Chapter Eight

I walked Ashley to her class after that. As I drifted off toward math class, I felt warm and fuzzy. Happy. I'd never felt like this before, and I was sure my gut reaction was right. Everything was going to be okay. Ashley and I would see this through.

After school, I tried to convince her to go back to the clinic with me.

I wanted to sit down and talk some more with Dr. Benson—more about pregnancy and about the possibility of not giving up the baby.

Ashley just shook her head. "I have to talk to my parents first. I owe them that."

All of a sudden that warm fuzzy feeling was gone. "I understand," I said. "Can I talk to them with you?"

"No," she said. "That wouldn't be good. I need to do this myself."

So I walked her home, but I didn't walk her up to her door.

That night, the shit hit the fan. The phone rang, and it was Ashley's father. He talked to my dad at first. All I could hear was the conversation on this end. My father was trying to be polite, but Mr. Walker must have been screaming. This was not good.

I heard my dad say finally in a nervous but controlled voice, "I'm sorry, I have to hang up now. Maybe we can have this conversation another time." And he hung up the phone.

Not a minute passed before the phone rang again. This time I picked it up in my room.

"Hi," I said. "It's me. Zach."

"Put your father back on the phone," he growled.

"No," I said. "I think it's me you need to talk to. Not him."

"Well, you are the source of the problem here."

"I know."

"What's this crazy idea you're putting in my daughter's head?" he asked.

"We're just trying to come to a decision that is right for us."

"Decision? Who are you to decide?"

I paused for a second. "I'm the father. I should have a say in this."

"You get my daughter pregnant and then tell me that you want to decide what's right for her future?" He was losing it now. I could hear it in his voice.

I was working hard at keeping my cool. My father walked into my room then and just stood there. "Put me back on the phone," he said. I shook my head no and then tried to ignore him.

I spoke slowly and carefully into the phone. "I want Ashley and me to decide together what comes next." And I probably should not have said what I said next. But he was pushing me. "Maybe the right thing is for her to have the baby and not give it up."

I waited for whatever was going to come next, but all I heard was a kind of ragged breathing into the phone. And then Mr. Walker slammed the receiver down.

My father was still standing there. I turned around to face him. And

I waited for him to say something. Maybe I even hoped he was going to say how proud he was of me for taking responsibility and also for not getting angry on the phone. Instead he just turned and walked away.

Chapter Nine

Soon everyone at school knew the situation. Or they knew at least that Ashley was pregnant and that I was the one who got her that way. Ashley had told Elisse and, well, Elisse told just about everyone. As you can imagine, there were various versions about how I got her pregnant.

Some of the guys I hardly knew were slapping me on the back. "Congratulations, dude," someone would say out of the blue as he walked down the hall giving me a thumbs-up. Actually, I don't think they were congratulating me. They were making fun of me. For Ashley's brother Stephen and his buddies, it was another story. No one actually did anything physical. It was always just a nasty look or someone saying, "We're watching you." Or Stephen's favorite line, "This isn't over yet."

The reaction from the girls was mixed as well. Some treated me like pond scum. Other girls who had never even paid attention to me would look my way in the hallway or in class. I could see that they were curious about me. I wasn't used to being the center of such attention.

And it seemed that every time I turned around, Kiley would show up and want to know how things were going. "Are you going to be all right?" she asked.

"Everything is going to turn out fine," I said.

"You are actually even considering having the baby? Don't you think Ashley would be too young to actually go through with this?"

"No," I said. "I think she'd be fine as long as I'm there to help."

"You mean it, don't you?"

"Well, we're considering the options," I said. I was becoming more certain every day that having the baby was the right way to go. I loved Ashley, and she loved me. All I needed, all Ashley and I needed, was for everyone to leave us alone.

Then Kiley gave me this really strange look. It didn't register at first, but after she walked away it clicked. It wasn't the kind of look that a friend gives you. It was more than that. And I discovered that I liked how that made me feel.

Ashley and I could hang out at the public library after school or in the park, but I wasn't allowed in her house, and her parents wouldn't let her come over to my house. When she was with me she seemed happy enough, but I could sense that she was more than a little scared. She had gotten used to being the pregnant girl in school. I was less than comfortable with my role, but I could handle it.

A couple of weeks passed, and we settled into a kind of "normal" routine. We'd gone back to Planned Parenthood a couple of times, and Ashley and I did a heck of a lot of talking about our situation. I'd also emailed back and forth with Mark for some of his thoughts. *Have the baby, dude. It will change your life*, he wrote once.

And then another week passed. And another. Ashley was hardly feeling sick at all, and kids had seemingly lost interest in our situation. We were old news. We were sitting in the library doing homework together when Ashley said, "You want this baby, don't you?"

"Yes," I finally said. "I want us to have the baby. I want to be there for you. And for the baby. I think we can do this."

Ashley was wide-eyed. She looked scared. "This doesn't seem like it's real."

I agreed. "I know. I find it hard to believe that by next year this time, we could both be parents of a little kid."

"That sounds so crazy," she said, but she was smiling now.

"Well, we've changed. We need to keep working at this."

"I know. It's just that sometimes I wish that things could go back to the way they used to be."

I hugged her then, and she cried softly into my shirt. Truth is, I had a million doubts about what we were doing. Would she be strong enough to go through with it? Would the baby be healthy? Would I be a good father? Would her parents allow me to be part of the picture? Did I really want to make this commitment? But something inside of me kept saying this was the right thing to do despite all the odds. I didn't say anything. I just closed my eyes and held her while the librarian at her desk looked over at us. But when she saw the frightened look on my face, she quickly looked away.

Chapter Ten

Strange as it may sound, both Ashley and I were doing better in school than we had been before she got pregnant. All that time hanging out together in the public library was paying off. We'd both cleaned up our act some. We stayed away from parties. Ashley knew she shouldn't drink or do anything that might affect the baby.

Yes, we started using those words: "the baby." Sometimes we referred to it as "our baby."

At home, my parents had backed off. They were worried, for sure, but they kept a lid on it. Not Ashley's parents. Ashley's dad called my father at least once a week. He wasn't screaming now, but he wasn't giving up. When he called, my father always walked the cordless phone into his bedroom and closed the door. And he never told me what they talked about. And I never asked.

But then I was blindsided.

I came home for dinner one night and saw Ashley's parents' car in the driveway. I walked into the house to find Ashley's mother and father sitting with my parents in the living room.

At first I just stood there. No one said a word. Mr. Walker looked like a bomb ready to explode. His wife looked like she'd been crying. My mother just looked down at the floor, and my father—well, he looked to me like some kind of traitor.

"What the hell is this?" I asked.

My father stood up. "I think it's time that we all sit down and talk about this together."

"This was my idea," Ashley's mother said timidly. "I persuaded your parents we should do this." Mrs. Walker was a shy woman who had rarely ever spoken to me the whole time I'd known Ashley.

"We all agree on one thing," my mother added. "Ashley is going to have the baby, and we need to do what is best for her and the child."

But I knew there was more to this. I didn't say a word. I was trying to keep control of my emotions. I felt like I was about to be bullied into something. I felt like I was being ganged up on.

Mr. Walker cleared his throat and took a deep breath. In a very controlled voice, he said, "Zach, do you know what an intervention is?"

I grimaced. "Yeah," I snorted. "When someone is out of control, when someone is on drugs, people get together and try to force that person to change." I paused and looked around at the faces in the room. "But no one is on drugs here. So what the hell is this?"

"We're here to help," Mrs. Walker said. "We want to help both Ashley and you."

"Why don't you sit down?" my mom said.

"I'd rather stand."

There was an awkward silence.

And then I heard the bathroom door open, and Ashley walked into the room. She looked like she wasn't feeling too well. "Hi, Zach," she said in a soft voice.

"Did you know about this?" I asked her.

She nodded.

"But I don't understand what's going on here," I said to her.

She sat down in an empty chair and fidgeted with her hands. "Zach, I've been having second thoughts about keeping the baby. Maybe we should give it up for adoption when it's born."

I felt rage rising up inside of me but knew I had to keep it together. I nodded at her parents. "They've been brainwashing you, haven't they?"

"No," she said. Her voice was weak, and I could tell this was incredibly hard for her. "I just don't think I'll be a very good mother."

"But I would be there to help," I said.

Ashley just looked away and stared at the wall. I glared at my own parents—the traitors who had allowed this scene. Then I glared at Mr. Walker. At that point I guess he couldn't contain himself.

"Yeah, Zach. And what kind of responsible father do you think you're going to be?" There was venom in his voice.

I knew I couldn't answer him. I was way too angry, and I'd regret whatever I said. I kept telling myself to keep it together. If I lost my cool, I knew that it would be playing right into what Ashley's father wanted.

Instead, I went over to Ashley and sat on the arm of the chair. I put my arm around her. Right then I wanted everything and everybody in the world to go away. I just wanted to be alone with Ashley.

"There are many women out there who can't have children," my mom said. "It would be like a dream come true for them to adopt a baby. The child would have a good life."

"A normal life," Mrs. Walker echoed.

My dad stood up. "We're going to go in the kitchen and leave you two to talk for a bit. Take your time. We're not trying to pressure you into anything." Those last words sounded hollow. This was so unlike him.

As they left the room, I felt trapped. For weeks I'd been pushing all of my own doubts into a closet. I knew a thousand reasons why we should not keep the baby. A million maybe. But I believed we could beat the odds, even get both sets of parents onside. And now this.

When they were gone, I sat down on the floor in front of Ashley, made her look me in the eye. "You okay?"

"I'm not feeling well," she said, "but I'm okay. I'm sorry about all this. It's partly my fault. I wanted all of us to sit down together and talk. I don't like having my parents hate you."

"But I thought we were okay with what we decided."

"I thought we were too. But it was more like what *you* had decided."

"We're in this together," I said.

"I know," she said. "But it's been a while since we actually talked about it. Do you still feel the same?"

The truth was, I had been thinking more and more that there would be so many impossible problems ahead. And I wasn't sure about how I could handle them. But in the end, I always convinced myself I could handle anything. I could do this. I wanted to be there as a good father. I could see it through.

"Yeah," I said. "More than ever."

Ashley nodded. "I guess I was thinking I needed to give you a way out."

"I don't want out."

"Okay," she said. "Then let's stick to our plan. I'll keep the baby. You'll be there to help, right?"

"I'll be there."

Chapter Eleven

We had about ten days of some kind of truce after that. Ashley's parents seemed to have backed off. So had mine. At school, we were still the center of attention whenever we were together. The school counselor had called us both in one day, but she was totally cool about the whole thing. She said that there would be a "plan" for Ashley so that she could stay in classes as long as she wanted and then do work from home when the time came. And, of course, she'd be back in school after she had the baby. It seemed like at least one person was on our side.

I had Ashley over to my house one night to watch a movie, and my parents seemed fine about that, even when they found us making out in the living room. And then Ashley invited me over to her house after school to study together there.

"I don't know if that's such a good idea," I said.

"Yes, it is. If we're going to make this work, my family is going to have to accept you."

"Yeah. Right."

"My dad won't be there," she said. "And Stephen has promised to get off your case."

So I did go to Ashley's house. We went there on the bus after school.

Her mom was a bit chilly but polite. Ashley made me coffee, and we sat in the kitchen and talked. Well, Ashley talked. Sometimes she became a real motormouth. And it wasn't like she was talking about us or the baby or our future or anything important. She was talking about what her friends were doing. There was Elisse's new boyfriend, who was from France, of all places. And Jessica, who had gone shopping at the mall. And Maya, who had a new crush on Liam. And about the parties that we had not been going to. And about which guys in which bands she thought were cute. And it went on and on. We sure didn't get much studying done.

As I sipped my coffee, I was beginning to realize just how young Ashley was. Even though we were just a year apart, I felt like it was much more than that. I felt so much older than her. What had happened? I felt like I was missing a piece of the puzzle here. What was I getting myself into with this girl?

Mrs. Walker walked in and boldly asked me if I wanted to stay for supper. I don't know whose jaw dropped farther, Ashley's or mine.

But I wasn't quite ready for that. Not the way I was feeling right then. "No thanks, Mrs. Walker," I said politely. "Not tonight. But I'll take a rain check."

"Sure. What's your favorite food? I could cook you something special. Just don't say pizza. I hate pizza."

I probably would have said pizza, but instead I lied, "Nah, I'm tired of pizza. What about lasagna?"

"Lasagna it is. You pick the night."

As I got up to go, I kissed Ashley right in front of her mom. I knew I had crossed over some kind of a bridge. But that wasn't exactly making me feel like a rock star. And, as I left the house, I found myself letting out a big lungful of air. Once I was beyond sight of Ashley's house, I started running, slowly at first but then faster until I was breathing hard. When I slowed down, I realized I hadn't even been running in the direction of home. I was down by the shops near the school. I slowed down by Java Junction and saw some of the kids from school inside. Sitting at a table by herself was Kiley. Kiley, who had been my girlfriend before I screwed things up. Kiley, who recently always seemed to be running into me in the hallways. Kiley, who right now was looking rather hot.

She wasn't looking this way. She was just sitting there staring into her cup, appearing to be rather lonely, while all around her other kids were in groups, laughing and having a good time. I thought about going in and just hanging with her for a while. I wanted someone to talk to. Someone other than Ashley.

But I didn't. I turned and walked away. I went home and sent an email to Mark in New Zealand. It went like this.

Yo, Mark. Do you ever have days when you feel like your freedom has been stolen from you? Do you wish like hell that you weren't a father? Do you learn to take flack from your girlfriend's parents? Do you feel like the rest of the world is out there having fun and your life looks like prison? Or is it all truly worth it? Tell me that being a father is the best damn thing on the planet.

Your buddy in North America,
Zach, Future Super Dad

Chapter Twelve

The next day at school, something clicked. Kiley was still running into me way too often. And something had changed about her. Her hair, her clothes. She'd always been a good-looking girl, but now something was different. And that way she looked at me. Honest, I tried to ignore it at first.

"I know what you're going through isn't easy, Zach. So I'm here for you any time if you want to talk. I've got a new cell. Here's the number." She slipped a piece of paper into my hand.

That night I got an email back from Mark.

Zach, dude. I don't know how to say this without sounding like the world's biggest turd. But that website thing— well, some of it is true. A lot of it is true, I guess. But, I mean, it was, like, this project we got a government grant to do. We told our stories, tried to put some smiley faces on the rough parts.

But fatherhood when you are this age is about as rough as it gets. Sure, the whole baby-being-born thing is great. But then it kicks in. You think flack from the girl's folks is the worst part? It isn't.

Losing your freedom is the worst of it. I can't believe how much I miss some of the silly stuff I used to do—just hanging with my mates and that sort of thing.

I had to stop reading then. This wasn't what I wanted to hear. Not now, not feeling the way I was already feeling. And that image of Kiley smiling at me kept popping up in my head. I swallowed hard.

And then I read the next line.

When I first started getting your emails, I thought it was, like, my role to encourage you. But now I know I was wrong. Dude, if you can bow out of this now, go for it. The world will not come crashing to an end. Sorry to have to say it, but there it is.

Your buddy in Kiwiland,
Mark

I woke up in a sweat that night. Why couldn't this all just be a bad dream? Why couldn't it all just go away? And why was this happening to me? By the next morning, however, I had decided to not let any of it get to me. Mark, whoever he was, was a jerk. How could he flaunt how great it was to be a father on a website, and then in those emails, and then, deep down, resent it? To hell with him. I had to be there for Ashley. I'd promised her that.

Breakfast was usually pretty quick at my house with my mom, dad and me burning toast and spilling coffee and not much talk. But my parents could see something was troubling me.

"Zach," my mom said, "I know this has all been pretty tough on you, but I think I'm actually quite proud of the way you're handling things."

"Most boys your age," my dad added, "wouldn't be willing to do what you're trying to do."

This should have been good news. My parents were trying to be supportive now. They'd done their best to change my mind, but now they'd accepted my decision.

"Thanks," I said. "It's very cool of you to say that."

"Let us know if there is anything we can do," my dad said as I put on my jacket and got ready to leave.

Just give me a new life, I wanted to say. Either that, or just fix it so I was never born.

At school that day, Ashley ran into me while I was talking to Kiley. I said goodbye to Kiley and walked Ashley to her class.

"She seems to be around an awful lot. What's with that?" Ashley asked.

"She's just a friend," I said. "And I don't have many friends."

"Yeah, but she's your old girlfriend."

"That's history. Now we're just friends," I said. "You feeling any better this morning?"

"About the same. I'm just getting used to it."

"Ashley, I'm ready to take up your mom on that dinner," I said.

"Lasagna, right?"

She phoned her mom on her cell and told her the news. It was a short conversation.

"And?" I asked.

"She's thrilled."

"I bet."

When I told my parents about eating at Ashley's, they once again said they were proud of me. I was turning into some kind of hero. And hating every minute of it.

I showed up right on time (as heroes should). Stephen greeted me at the door. Well, he opened the door and scowled. I could smell that something was burning. Mr. and Mrs. Walker were arguing in the kitchen. Stephen just walked away, and I was left standing there. Ashley came down the stairs looking a little more pale than usual. She hugged me and nodded toward the kitchen. "Mom burned the lasagna."

We sat on the sofa and watched the news. Eventually Ashley's parents emerged from the kitchen.

"A minor disaster," her dad said. "We've phoned for pizza though."

"I'm okay with pizza," I said, smiling.

Mrs. Walker looked flustered, and her face was flushed. "I'm glad you came, Zach."

"Nice to be here," I said politely.

I'd like to say that everything went smoothly after that.

But it didn't.

It took almost an hour for the pizza to arrive. And it was not the one they ordered.

It was cold and had anchovies, which nobody liked. I think Stephen had been smoking some weed in his room, and when he came downstairs he was acting a little funny. He didn't actually say anything to me, just gave me looks that could paralyze.

Mrs. Walker tried to tell funny stories about when Ashley was young, but Ashley kept asking her to stop.

While we were eating, Mr. Walker flatly announced, "This is the worst pizza I've ever had. I'm going to call and complain." Being agitated seemed to be his style.

"Don't," Mrs. Walker said and then turned to me. "Sorry about the meal, Zach."

I shrugged. "It's okay."

"You don't need to apologize to him," Mr. Walker said.

Stephen let out a snorting laugh.

I kept trying to offer up some small talk about school or sports, but it went nowhere. It seemed that whatever I said, Ashley's father had something negative to say about it. Pretty soon I knew I'd made a mistake by coming over and trying to be nice to her family.

After about five minutes of dead silence, I found myself saying, "Why don't we cut through some of the crap and just talk about the baby." I didn't mean for it to sound hostile. I thought it would help if we could just get it out in the open. But it came out sounding all wrong.

Mr. Walker looked up from his plate. "Good point, Zach. Yes, let's do just that. Why don't you start us off?"

Mrs. Walker was shaking her head. Ashley looked paler than ever. I didn't know where to begin.

I guess my silence was another wrong response, because Stephen was out of his seat now. "Yeah, why don't we cut through the crap," he said. And then he leaned across the table and shoved me hard with both hands.

"Sit down," his father ordered him.

I was trying to stay calm. I slowly started to stand. I figured I'd better just leave. Ashley took my hand, but I pulled away. "No, I think I better be going."

"I'm so sorry," Mrs. Walker said again.

"Mom, you don't need to apologize," Stephen said.

I couldn't believe this was happening. All I wanted was to get out of there.

But I didn't make it to the door. Stephen said, "Good riddance to bad trash," and then pushed me hard from behind so that I slammed into the wall.

I wasn't even thinking. Just reacting. I turned and pushed him. I pushed him so hard that he fell backward over a table. Some framed pictures fell to the floor, and then Stephen hit the floor. Hard. I didn't hang around to see what might happen next. I was out the door and walking quickly away into the cold night air.

Chapter Thirteen

Ashley wouldn't speak to me the next day at school. I couldn't believe things had gone from bad to worse. I waited for her outside several of her classes, but she refused to even look at me or make eye contact. I had to talk with her. I thought she would have realized that none of what happened was my fault. But all she said was, "Just leave me alone. Haven't you done enough damage?"

I felt rotten. Really rotten.

I saw Stephen in the hall, and I could see he had a big bruise on his face. I thought about trying to apologize, but I knew it wouldn't work. And I wouldn't be surprised if he tried to hit me. Then we'd end up in more trouble, and I sure didn't want that, or any more attention.

It was one of my worst days of school ever. I couldn't concentrate and I couldn't figure out how to patch things up. After school was finished, I was sitting in the back of the bus thinking about what a crappy future I had ahead of me when Kiley sat down beside me.

"You don't look so good," she said.

I told her what had happened.

She didn't say anything at first. "Maybe this just isn't meant to be," she finally said. I knew exactly what she meant.

"I don't know what it is," I said. "I've been trying to do the right thing."

"Maybe you're trying to do the wrong thing. I know your heart is in the right place. It just seems that it's not working out."

I knew there was more to this than what Kiley was saying. I could see it in her face. It was that look she had given me back when we had first gotten together. We'd been together for almost a year, and then I screwed things up. After that, Ashley had come along, and the rest, as they say, is history.

But maybe Kiley was right. Maybe Mark was right. And my parents. And Ashley's parents. Maybe everyone could see things clearly but me. When it was time for Kiley to get off the bus, she said, "Call me if you need someone to talk to. I'll be there for you."

Both of my parents' cars were in the driveway when I got home. That was weird. They both should have been at work. I knew something was up. But I would never have expected what happened next.

I walked into the kitchen, and my father was reading some kind of document. He looked up at me. "What happened last night, Zach?"

I looked down at the floor. "Ashley's brother and I had a little disagreement."

"Maybe not so little?" he asked.

"Why?"

"This," he said, holding out the pages in his hands. "It's a restraining order. The Walkers went to the police, and they delivered this today. You're not allowed to have any contact with Stephen or Ashley."

"This is crazy," I said. "It wasn't my fault. They can't do this."

My mother came up to me then and put her arm around me. "If they went this far, this is very serious. Zach, I think you just have to back off. I think you have to let all this go."

"This is so unfair."

My dad set the papers on the table. "I don't think you have much of a choice here, Zach. I think you need to let Ashley and her parents sort out whatever they're going to do. Anything you try to do now would only make things worse."

"And you could get in real trouble," my mom said, the look of parental worry stamped on her forehead.

"Maybe this is all for the best," my dad said. And that was the last thing I wanted to hear.

Chapter Fourteen

I called Ashley's cell phone nearly a dozen times, but she didn't pick up. She would have known it was me calling. I realized that doing even this was going against the restraining order, but I didn't care. All I wanted to do was talk to her and find out what she was thinking and feeling. I needed to know what was going on.

It was almost midnight when I called Kiley. She had been sleeping, but she listened to me and she had some kind words for me. I eventually let her go and then fell into a fitful sleep.

In the morning, I got another reminder from my parents about leaving Ashley alone. "We don't want this legal thing to get any worse. Zach, you just have to back off. That's all you can do."

And that's what I did. I backed off.

I didn't get on the bus at the corner. The weather was a bit cooler, and it looked like rain, but I walked for ten blocks and then put out my thumb. Hitchhiking out of town was much more difficult this time. I did a lot of walking by the side of the highway, and the fact that so many drivers ignored me made me feel more and more like crap. Finally, a guy in an old beat-up Toyota stopped and picked me up and talked the whole time about what a rotten life he had. But he gave me a long drive to the exit I wanted, and then I walked the rest of the way to the river I'd been to before. I felt confused and tired as I sat down. I had never felt more alone in my life. But at least I *was* alone. I didn't have anyone there telling me what to do or think. I thought about Ashley, and now I didn't know if it was worth it. It would always be like this. Her parents would be there telling her what she should do. And no matter how hard I would try, they'd always, always resent me. They'd want me out of the picture.

Ashley and I had said we "loved" each other. But now I was even less certain that I knew what love was. I was even more confused by the way I was feeling when I was around Kiley. Kiley seemed so much more mature than Ashley.

I remembered the day I'd been here before and was reminded of that other option: running away. Just splitting and leaving it all behind. It seemed so sweet.

But again, I couldn't do it to my parents.

I tried to focus on the baby that Ashley would have: what that would be like and what I would be like as a father. But I couldn't see it. I couldn't bring that picture into focus in my head.

And then it started to rain. I tucked in beneath a rock outcropping on the hill above the falls and watched the rain coming down. I was cold and damp and alone. After about two hours, I felt like I was going crazy. I had this big temptation to call Kiley. But I didn't. I checked my watch and waited until I knew Ashley would be between classes. No one was supposed to have their cell phone on at school, but almost everyone did. I blocked my number and phoned Ashley.

She picked up.

As I looked out at the rainy dismal world around me, I said, "Please don't hang up."

She didn't say anything, but she didn't hang up.

"I just want to know if you still care about me."

"I do, Zach. It's just that now everything is so impossible."

"You know I didn't mean to hurt your brother."

"I know that. But it's just not going to work between us. My parents are right. I just have to admit it. You have to admit it."

"I know it's bad, but did they have to get the police involved?"

"What?" She sounded genuinely surprised.

"You didn't know?"

"Know what?"

"About the restraining order. I'm not allowed to even see you or speak with you. I can be in big trouble just for talking to you on the phone like this."

"That's crazy. My parents did this?"

"Yeah, I'm afraid so."

Then there was silence. I was aware of the sound of the falling rain and the waterfall. I guess Ashley heard it too.

"Zach, where are you?"

"I just had to get away. I hitchhiked to this place up in the mountains. I couldn't handle going to school."

"Are you all right?"

"I think so. Everything is just so insane."

"We need to talk," she said. "Some place where no one will see us."

"I'll hitch back to town. If I leave now I might get back by the time school is out. Meet me in the bookstore over on South Park Street, the one with the coffee shop. I think it's called Off the Page. Do you know where that is?"

"Okay, I'll be there."

The rain let up, but I had a long walk before I caught my first ride. It took me longer than I thought it would to get back to town. Maybe my career as a hitchhiker was over. Ashley had been in the bookstore waiting for me for over an hour. But she hadn't given up.

When I walked in, she ran to me and gave me a hug.

I could tell she was just as scared as I was. We talked for a long time. And then she said it was time for us to go talk to her parents.

Chapter Fifteen

We took the city bus. As we got closer to her house, I started to lose my nerve. I was cold and tired and even a bit shaky.

"I've thought about being pregnant and about the baby so many times," Ashley confided. "And each time I get more confused. I'm not ready for this."

"I don't think I am either," I admitted.

"But we both decided that you'd have the baby, right?"

"I don't want to change that. I still think that's the right thing for me to do. I just don't know about us."

"What do you mean?"

"I don't know about you and me being parents."

"I've thought about that too. Some days I feel confident that we can do it. Other times it really scares me."

She saw the uncertainty in my face. Right now she seemed the stronger of the two of us, the one who was more mature. "What are we going to say to your parents?" I asked.

"I don't know," she said. And suddenly I wished we weren't about to go through with this meeting.

All too soon we were back in Ashley's neighborhood, and the bus stopped. We got out and walked to her door.

When we walked in, the house was quiet. We sat down in the living room, and Ashley's mom came in first. She looked at me and then at Ashley. "He's not supposed to be here," she said.

"Mom, you had no right to get the police involved. It wasn't Zach's fault. Stephen pushed him first."

Ashley's mom shook her head. "It was your father's idea. I shouldn't have gone along with it."

"Is he home yet?" Ashley asked.

"He should be here any minute," Mrs. Walker said. She turned to me and added, "I'm not sure it's such a good idea that you are here."

I shrugged and looked at Ashley. "Do you want me to leave?"

"No," she said emphatically.

A few awkward minutes later, we heard the car in the driveway and the sound of Mr. Walker's footsteps. Then the door opened, and he walked in.

He glared at me and at Ashley and, without saying anything, started walking to the phone. He picked it up, but his wife marched over and made him put it down.

He stood there and tried to contain his anger. "What are you doing here?" he asked me.

"I don't know," I said. "I just know that we need to sort this out."

"It was my idea," Ashley said. "Why didn't you tell me about the restraining order?"

He didn't answer.

"You need to call the police and tell them you made a mistake," Ashley demanded.

"I'm not going to do that."

"I've been thinking about how you are controlling my life, and I don't think it's fair."

"You are too young to know what fair is," he snapped. "And you don't know what's right for you."

"I need a chance to figure that out."

"And how are you going to do that?"

Ashley was being more assertive around her parents than I'd seen her before, but she was also looking flustered. "I think Zach and I just need to go away together for a while."

This was not at all what I was expecting her to say.

Her father seethed silently as her mother said, "We don't want you to do that. We want you here."

I knew what Ashley was thinking. I'd thought about it before. We'd talked about it. It had always been an option. Running away. But it was all wrong.

"No, Ashley," I said in a soft voice. "We're not going to run away together. We're not going to do that. I've already done the rehearsals on that. It's not the way to go."

"Then what is the way to go?" her father demanded.

I looked at Ashley and thought of all the conversations she and I had about the pregnancy and the baby. I knew what we needed. We needed more time.

"Look," I said, "I think everyone needs to back off and let us have a chance to think it through." I looked her father right in the eye. "You don't have to like me, but you might just have to get used to having me around. I'd like to be here for Ashley, unless she tells me she doesn't want me around. I'd also like to be there for the baby, even though I'm not at all sure if I'd be any good at helping out with that."

"Have you thought any more about giving the baby up for adoption when it's born?" Ashley's mom asked.

"We've talked about it as a possibility," Ashley said.

"I don't think it's what I want," I said. "But I haven't ruled it out. I just know that there are no easy answers here."

Mr. Walker looked at me differently now. The hostility had faded. It's almost like he was looking at me as me for the first time, not as the boy who had gotten his daughter pregnant. "Well, you sure got that part right," he said.

And that's where we left it. I gave Ashley a hug and walked home. I was still baffled as to what would come next. I didn't know how we were going to sort out the difficulties or make the right decision. All I knew was that we had, for now, taken some control. There would be problems ahead and difficult decisions. And I knew I would never be fully prepared for what lay ahead. But we had taken our lives back for now. There would be a child, and we'd have to figure out what would be best for that child.

Maybe Ashley and I could see it through and stay together. It wouldn't be easy. Nothing would be easy from here on. But I knew one thing for sure. I'd be there for her right up to the time the baby was born and beyond. We'd see this through together.

Lesley Choyce teaches part-time at Dalhousie University, runs Pottersfield Press and has published over seventy books for adults and kids. He surfs year-round in the North Atlantic and has been a newspaper boy and lead guitarist. Lesley lives at Lawrencetown Beach, Nova Scotia.

orca soundings

The following is an excerpt from
another exciting Orca Soundings novel,
Comeback by Vicki Grant.

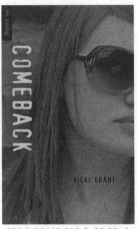

978-1-55469-310-8 $9.95 pb
978-1-55469-311-5 $16.95 lib

RIA IS RICH, SLIM, PRETTY, POPULAR.

If you only knew her at school, you'd think she
led a charmed life. But her situation has suddenly
changed. Her parents' seemingly perfect marriage
has broken up, and before she's had a chance to
absorb the blow, her father disappears in a plane
crash. What's worse, rumors begin to surface that
he may not be the man—or father—everyone
thought he was. Ria decides she needs to take
desperate action to protect herself, her younger
bother and her father's reputation.

Chapter One

My boyfriend is trying to make me feel better. He's leaning against his locker, one arm over my head, making a little cocoon for me. He tucks a wisp of hair behind my ear and says, "It's not the end of the world, Ria. Who knows? You might even end up liking it. So smile, would you? C'mon. Just a little… Please?"

I appreciate the effort. I really do. Colin's sweet—but it's not helping. He doesn't know how I feel.

How could he?

His life's right off the Disney Channel. The mom. The dad. The three kids. The mischievous but lovable dog. Everyone sitting around the kitchen table, laughing at dumb jokes and flicking corn Niblets at each other.

Colin couldn't possibly understand what it's like to live without all that—any more, I guess, than I could have three months ago.

The weird thing is I didn't even know my life was perfect until suddenly it just wasn't anymore. It was like waking up after a car crash and realizing your legs aren't there. Who even thinks about how great walking is before something like that happens?

The word *crippled* pops into my head, and that's enough to get me started again. I have to close my eyes.

Colin says, "Oh, no. Ria…" I feel the air go out of him.

This isn't fair. I shouldn't make him miserable just because I am. That's the type of thing my mother would do.

What am I saying? That's the type of thing my mother *did* do.

This whole thing is all about *her*. *Her* life, *her* happiness, *her* whatever.

It's as if one morning she just decided she didn't want to be married anymore, and that was that. No explanation. No apology. No nothing.

Next thing we knew, she'd kicked Dad out. She'd fired the housekeeper, cut up our credit cards, took a pathetic little job at an office somewhere and jammed the freezer full of these Styrofoam disks that she insists on calling pizza.

I don't get it. If we're suddenly so poor, why won't she cash the checks Dad keeps leaving for her? He's a big stockbroker. He's got tons of money. He doesn't mind giving it to us. He *wants* to.

Mom's trying to embarrass him. That's what she's doing. She knows it's going to look bad for him to be wining and dining his clients at the best restaurants in town when his own kids can't even "afford" take-out pizza anymore.

I'm sure I sound mad and childish and spoiled—and I probably am—but I can't help it. When this whole thing started, I tried to be supportive. I choked down the frozen pizza. I didn't complain when Mom canceled our trip to Italy. I looked after my little brother Elliot. I even attempted to be sympathetic.

I mean, I'm not totally blind. I can see Dad isn't the easiest guy to be married to. He's away on business too much. He's involved in too many organizations. He's got too many friends, clients, acquaintances, whatever—and they all want to go golfing with him.

I can understand how that would get to Mom.

I figured she just needed a break. After a couple of weeks—and maybe jewelry and a romantic dinner somewhere—she'd remember the good things about Dad, and then we could all just go back to being a family again. That's what I thought.

At least until this morning, when I found out Mom went and sold our house. Now, on top of everything, she's making us move into some gross little condo, miles from all our friends and our schools and—oh, yeah, what a coincidence—our father.

I can't be sympathetic anymore. This is her midlife crisis. We shouldn't all have to suffer from it.

I'm not going to be like that.

I open my eyes and smile at Colin. "I'm fine," I say. "My contacts were just bothering me."

There's no way Colin believes that, but by this point, he's probably had enough of my honesty. He kisses me on the forehead and then starts manhandling me toward the cafeteria. I laugh as if it's all fun and games, but I'm not sure how long I can keep up the act. The thought of having to do my Miss Congeniality thing for the entire lunch-eating population of Citadel High exhausts me.

My phone rings just as we get to the burger lineup. Ms. Meade glares at me and says, "Cell phones. Outside." Normally, I think that rule's totally unfair, but today it strikes me as proof that God just might exist after all. I mumble "Sorry" and slip out the side door onto the parking lot. I can see Colin is torn between keeping an eye on me and placing his order, but he follows me out anyway.

"Hey," I say into the phone.

"Hello, Princess."

"Dad!" I smile for real. I can't remember the last time I did that. "Where are you?"

"Guess."

I don't have to. Colin has already spotted him and is dogging it across the parking lot toward the biggest, shiniest old convertible I've ever seen. It's turquoise and white and has these giant Batmobile fins on the back. Dad's leaning up against it. He's got his tie loosened and his jacket slung over one shoulder as if he's auditioning for *Mad Men*.

I have to laugh. "Where did you get that thing?"

"Thing?! I'll have you know this vehicle once belonged to Elvis Presley."

"Dad."

"Seriously! And Elvis always had a gorgeous redhead in the passenger seat. So hurry up, darlin'. The King's waiting."

By this time, a kid I recognize from my English class has wandered over to check out the car too. Dad gives us the guided tour—the whitewall tires, the original upholstery, the engine, even the ashtrays. I don't know anything about cars, but I can see it's impressing the hell out of the two boys.

Dad basks in the glory for a while, then tosses Colin the keys. "Okay, big guy, let's blow this pop stand."

Colin looks at the keys, looks back at Dad, then yelps like a cowboy. He jumps into the driver's seat.

The other kid starts walking away, but Dad goes, "Whoa. Stop. You too. Get in."

The kid kind of laughs and says, "No. Thanks. That's okay." He tries to slink away, but Dad's not taking no for an answer.

"Life's too short to miss riding in a gen-u-ine mint-condition 1962 LeSabre ragtop." Dad points at the car as if he's sending the kid to the principal's office. "Now hop in, boy! I mean it."

The kid looks at me for help. I shake my head. What can I do? When my father wants something, he gets it.

You can tell the kid's worried there's a hidden camera somewhere, but he shrugs and climbs in the backseat with Dad anyway. I slide in beside Colin. We take off with a screech.

Dad doesn't tell Colin to slow down and doesn't freak out when he comes a tad too close to a parked car. He just reaches over the front seat and cranks up the radio. The wind whips my hair over my mouth and eyes. Colin's hat flies off. People on the sidewalk turn to watch us. We're all hooting and laughing. It's so perfect. It's almost like we're in a commercial.

This whole thing is Classic Dad. The surprise visit at the exact right time.

The amazing car that may or may not have belonged to Elvis Presley. Letting Colin drive. Dragging a stranger along. Turning an ordinary Friday lunch period into something pretty close to a "life moment."

So maybe it's a bit on the flashy side. What's wrong with that? Dad's right. Life is too short not to enjoy it. I'm only seventeen, and I get that. Why doesn't Mom?

I turn around and look at Dad. He's making Tim or Tom—I don't remember the guy's name—sing the doo-wop part of some old rock-and-roll song. The fact that neither of them knows the tune doesn't bother him at all. They're hollering at the top of their lungs like two kids at a campfire.

It's right then that I realize something.

I know how I can fix this thing.

I suddenly know how we can all be happy again.

orca soundings

The following is an excerpt from
another exciting Orca Soundings novel,
Rock Star by Adrian Chamberlain.

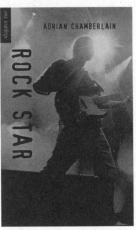

978-1-55469-235-4 $9.95 pb
978-1-55469-236-1 $16.95 lib

STRUGGLING AT HOME AND AT SCHOOL,
Duncan decides to try out for a local rock band.
He plays the bass guitar in the school orchestra,
but it is a long way from band camp to rock
star. Joining a heavy-metal band, he tries to fit
in, dumping his old friends and trying to walk
the walk. When his dad's new girlfriend starts to
teach him about real rock music and introduces
him to her musician brother, Duncan discovers
that there is more to being a guitar hero than
playing in a heavy-metal band.

Chapter One

After school I walk up the front steps of our house and head straight for the kitchen. I'm starving. There's a peanut butter jar on the counter. But sure enough, someone's used it all up. Empty. That puts me in a bad mood.

There's almost nothing in the fridge. Some stuff that looks like dog food in a Tupperware container. Milk. Old celery.

I grab the celery and take a bite. Ugh. All wilty and squishy. So I bend over and gob it into the garbage bin. This is disgusting and weirdly satisfying at the same time.

I'm still bent over the garbage when Dad calls me into the living room.

"Duncan!" he yells. "Duncan!"

You'd think I was twelve or something, not fifteen. I'm in grade ten.

School's not my favorite thing, to tell you the truth. Mostly it's boring. Some days I even hate it.

But one thing I do like is the school band. I play bass guitar. Sure, the songs are pretty lame. What do you expect from a big orchestra, with clarinets and French horns and all that stuff? But playing bass guitar is pretty cool.

It's just me and Dad now. I don't have brothers and sisters or anything. Mom died two years ago. She had cancer. It was quick. One day she sat down with me to tell me. She'd been sick for a while, and the doctors thought it was something else at first. I forget what. But then they figured out it was cancer. Six weeks later, she was dead.

"Duncan McCann! Can you come in here for a second?"

I stop gagging and stand there, motionless, like a video on pause. I thought the house was empty. Something in Dad's voice sounds different. I remain still. I've got a pretty good imagination. If I pretend something, I can even forget what I was doing before. Five seconds go by. Then I walk into the living room. There's this blond lady sitting on the couch with Dad. Weird. Unbelievable. And Dad looks kind of nervous or something. Even though he's smiling.

"Duncan, I'd like to introduce you to Terry. She's a friend of mine," says Dad.

"Hey, Duncan," the lady says. She's smiling. She's taller than Mom was. And sort of all-right-looking for an older lady. Dad's fifty. And Terry's probably forty or something. She's wearing a leather jacket. Mom would never have worn a leather jacket. Not in a million years.

"Hi," I say. I'm still holding my backpack. I drop it on the wood floor. It weighs a ton and makes a loud noise, like a kick drum.

"Yes. So anyway, Duncan. You'll be seeing a bit of Terry around the house. I mean, we're…well, seeing each other. She and I."

I was getting it now. Dad has a girl-friend. This lady. She smiles and holds out her hand.

"Okay," I say, shaking her hand. Then I pick up my pack and run upstairs to my room. I slam the door. I fall on my bed, face into my pillow, which sort of smells like corn chips. I'm not crying. I mean, I'm fifteen years old now. I'm not crying, but I feel like it.

After a while, I turn over. My face is still hot, but I feel better. I look around and—this may sound dumb—but I pretend I'm all alone on a desert island. Like I'm washed up on the beach, waking up with the tropical sun beating on my back. Then I look up. The walls of my room are mostly covered with posters of bands. I'm crazy about music. There's one of Death Cab for Cutie. An old Beastie Boys poster.

There's also a painting on the wall that my mom made. It's of a cabin by Shawnigan Lake. We once rented it for two weeks one summer. I was ten. That was my best summer. We swam in the lake almost every day. When I dived down, I could see green shafts of sunlight underwater. After swimming, me and my friend Jason would go to the corner store to buy candy. We walked in the dirt beside the road. Brown powdery dust squished up between my toes. Sounds dumb now, but back then I thought that was the greatest.

I've got Mom's beat-up old record player on my desk. I've got all her records too. She liked the Beatles a lot. I put on her favorite song. It's called "Here, There and Everywhere." It's a sappy ballad, but I like it. I think about Dad and this Terry lady, then about Mom. And then—I'm embarrassed to admit it—I start crying. For real. Blubbering all over the place. What a loser.

My cell phone buzzes. It's Jason's number. I don't answer. I don't feel like talking. Instead, I go back to pretending I'm on that desert island. I'm facedown on the bed, pretending my ship has gone down. It's late morning, and the sun's killing my back. Pretty soon I've gotta get up and build my shelter. Maybe find some food. Like turtle eggs. I read once how some guy on a desert island had to eat turtle eggs. Would that be like chicken eggs? Probably not.

I roll over, kind of slip-sliding off my bed onto the floor. Then I get my bass guitar out of the closet. Put the record-player needle back to the beginning of "Here, There and Everywhere" and start to play along. It sounds all right. I got my bass about a year ago. Actually, Dad bought it for me. But for a long time I didn't feel like learning to play it. I was pretty depressed. I even had to go to a psychiatrist for a while. Dad was worried about me because I got real sad after Mom died. For a while, I didn't want to get out of bed. Maybe for, like, two weeks. After that, Dad made me go to that stupid shrink.

After "Here, There and Everywhere," I try to play along with some other songs on the Beatles record. But it doesn't sound as good. Then I hear Dad yelling from downstairs for me to set the table. That's one of my jobs. Also, I clean one of the bathrooms every weekend, take out the garbage and sometimes help Dad make dinner.

Terry has gone home, so it's just me and Dad at dinner.

"Duncan," he says, dabbing his lips with a napkin. "Did you know Terry is a bank teller?"

"Nope," I say.

"Yes. She's quite an interesting lady. We were, you know, talking about films. Movies. And her favorites are…let me remember. Oh yes. *When Harry Met Sally*. And that other one, you know, about that large ship that hits an iceberg."

"*Titanic*," I say. I cram some peas into my mouth. How can Dad not know that?

He goes on to tell me that Terry lives in Esquimalt, which is part of Victoria, where we live. I don't ask Dad one thing about Terry. I'm kind of mad or confused or something, which is actually how I feel a lot of the time. It's like my emotions boil up and it's hard to control them. Weird, I know.

I help do the dishes after supper. Dad talks a lot about some guys at his work, and who said what to who and what so-and-so thought about so-and-so. It sounds mean, but I wish he'd shut up, because it's incredibly boring. But I don't want to hurt his feelings, so I just dry the dishes and say nothing.

I go back up to my room, leaving Dad to watch some dumb TV show. Something about monkeys. Dad is crazy about nature shows. If there's a monkey or a giraffe or a lion or a koala bear on TV, he has to watch it. I like action movies—like James Bond movies or *Collateral*—or shows about police detectives trying to solve old murders. Cold cases, they're called. I like it best when they dig up an old skull or hold up the rusty, crappy old hammer some maniac used to kill some poor guy, or when they look at a bloodstained pillowcase under a microscope. I guess that's sort of weird. But I make no apologies.

I put the Beatles record back on and play along to "Here, There and Everywhere" again. Then I get under my covers, not even taking my clothes off. I shut my eyes, sniff my smelly old corn-chip pillow and pretend I'm on that desert island again, thinking about those turtle eggs. They'd be all mushy inside, right? But, hey, you gotta eat to survive.

After a while my thoughts get all confused. You know how it is just before you fall asleep, and your mind starts to go into free fall, where anything goes?

From the desert island I go back to that summer at Shawnigan Lake, swimming in the green water with sunlight shafting into the deeper brown-black water. Some big dark fish are down below— it's scary for some reason. And then I'm dreaming…dreaming that I'm sinking deeper and deeper, and that I can still see the sunlight. But it's far, far above. And then I'm asleep.

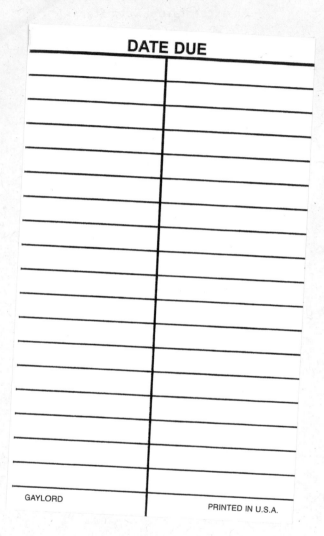